BIONICLE®

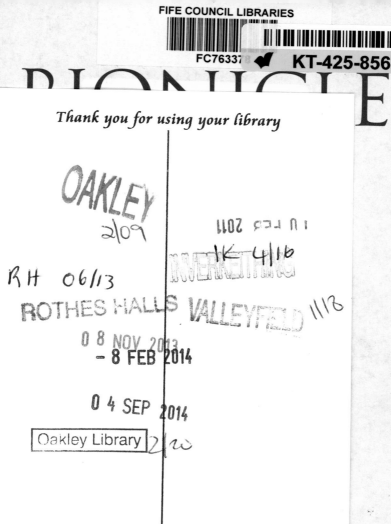

FIFE COUNCIL WEST AREA	
763378	
PETERS	30-Mar-07
JF	£3.99
JACT	DB

This book was first published in 2007 by Scholastic Inc.
First published in Great Britain in 2007 by HarperCollins Children's Books.
HarperCollins Children's Books is a division of HarperCollins Publishers Ltd.
1 3 5 7 9 10 8 6 4 2
LEGO, the LEGO logo and BIONICLE are trademarks of the LEGO Group.
©2007 The LEGO Group. All rights reserved.
Produced by HarperCollins Publishers Ltd. under license from the LEGO Group and
published by arrangement with Scholastic Inc., 557 Broadway, New York, NY, USA.
www.BIONICLE.com
ISBN-13: 978-0-00-724631-1
ISBN-10: 0-00-724631-5
A CIP catalogue for this title is available from the British Library.

The HarperCollins website address is:
www.harpercollinschildrensbooks.co.uk
Printed and bound in Great Britain.

This book is proudly printed on paper which contains wood
from well managed forests, certified in accordance with
the rules of the Forest Stewardship Council.
For more information about FSC,
please visit www.fsc-uk.org

Mixed Sources
Product group from well-managed
forests and other controlled sources
www.fsc.org Cert no. SW-COC-1806
© 1996 Forest Stewardship Council

Characters

Island of Metru Nui
THE TURAGA
Dume Elder of Metru Nui

Nuju

Vakama

Nokama   Former Toa Metru

Onewa   and Turaga of the

Whenua   villages of the island

Matau   of Mata Nui

THE MATORAN
Jaller A Ta-Matoran villager, now serving as captain of the Ta-Metru Guard

Matoro Ko-Matoran aide to Turaga Nuju

THE TOA
Takanuva Toa of Light

Tahu Nuva Toa Nuva of Fire

Gali Nuva Toa Nuva of Water

Pohatu Nuva Toa Nuva of Stone

Onua Nuva Toa Nuva of Earth

Lewa Nuva Toa Nuva of Air

Kopaka Nuva Toa Nuva of Ice

Island of Voya Nui
<u>THE MATORAN</u>

Garan Onu-Matoran leader
of the resistance
Balta Ta-Matoran, able to improvise
tools from anything lying around
Kazi Ko-Matoran with many secrets
Velika Po-Matoran inventor
Dalu Ga-Matoran fighter
Piruk Le-Matoran, skilled in stealth

<u>THE PIRAKA</u>

Zaktan Emerald-armoured
leader of the Piraka
Hakann Crimson-armoured Piraka
Reidak Ebony-armoured Piraka
Avak Tan-armoured Piraka
Thok White-armoured Piraka
Vezok Blue-armoured Piraka

*   *   *

INTRODUCTION

Zaktan, leader of the Piraka, paused on the top step of the stone staircase. If the information he had been given was correct, there were a total of 777 of these steps, all leading down to a vast chamber. Inside that chamber was the fabled Mask of Life, an artifact so powerful even the mighty Brotherhood of Makuta had never dared try to seize it for themselves.

Of course, if all it took to get it was walking down a staircase, any Matoran villager could have gotten his hands on it years ago. No, the stairs were guarded, the chamber was guarded, and no doubt the mask was guarded as well.

Is there anything in this miserable universe that isn't guarded? Zaktan wondered.

Despite the dangers, the Piraka would make the journey and do their best to obtain the mask, through fair means or foul. It was what they did, after all.

Toa perform senseless acts of "heroism" that benefit them not in the slightest, Zaktan said to himself. *Matoran labor ceaselessly until they drop dead with an idiotic smile of satisfaction on their lips. And Piraka steal things other beings want.*

It was a good existence, if a dangerous one. There were plenty of opportunities to increase one's personal wealth while engaging in random acts of destruction. And never underestimate the fun of exploiting lesser species, sparking environmental disasters, or ending the existence of the occasional Toa, all in the name of profit.

Not that everything was cracked Kanohi and wailing Matoran, he had to admit that. The Piraka had once been members of the secretive and extremely vicious organisation known as the Dark Hunters. After centuries of stealing, burning, kidnapping, and other activities on behalf of the group and its leader, the Shadowed One, the Piraka had decided to strike out on their own. This guaranteed a death sentence from their former employer.

But when we get the Mask of Life, Zaktan thought, *we will see about that sentence — and just who will live and who will die.*

The idea sparked memories of the days that he and the other Piraka had spent as Dark Hunters. It was a period of time he tried not to think about, for personal — and painful — reasons. After all, when he first joined the Shadowed One's service, he had been a whole being. Now he was a mass of squirming, buzzing, microscopic protodites, a monster in the eyes of even his fellow Piraka.

Against his will, his thoughts flew back to the past, his own and that of the other Piraka. Some of the memories were of things he himself had lived, others based on tales told by Hakann, Vezok, and the rest. Together, they formed a dark tapestry, a legacy of evil, that had now brought the six Piraka to the very brink of total victory.

Zaktan continued down the massive stairway, and remembered....

ONE

Seven Thousand Years Ago...

Hakann dug his fingers into the side of the cliff and cursed. Crumbling rock and gusts of icy wind threatened to dislodge him from his precarious perch. A Toa on patrol up above might, at any moment, look over the side and spot him. And then, of course, there was that 3,000-bio drop to the river below....

Still, Hakann had included all of that in his plan. His real problem was the dead weight hanging onto his ankle. Worse, the dead weight was loud and had a name: Vezok.

"I knew this was a bad idea!" Hakann's companion shouted, trying to be heard over the wind.

"A little louder!" Hakann snapped. "I think there might be a Toa somewhere who didn't hear you!"

"You said this would be a quick smash-and-snatch," Vezok continued, lowering his voice not at all. "In and out. You didn't say anything about climbing sheer cliffs in the middle of a battle and breaking into a Toa fortress!"

"I forgot," Hakann muttered. "If you're unhappy, Vezok, you can always let go. I'll make sure to let your friends — if you have any — know where to look for your pieces."

It was a good plan, Hakann knew, but unfortunately one that needed two thieves to pull off. The Toa who had built a base on this barren, windswept rock had neglected to inspect the icebergs that surrounded it. If they had done so, they would have discovered those chunks of ice were in fact camouflage for a tribe of Frostelus. Miserable, ill-smelling and ill-tempered creatures, Frostelus were happy to invade your territory but hated it when you invaded theirs. They had massed an army and promptly besieged the Toa.

The Matoran trader who passed this

information on to Hakann also said that the Toa planned to smuggle their "treasure" off the island within a few nights. Since the only exit not blocked by Frostelus was down the cliffside, Hakann reasoned the treasure had to be something light and easily carried. He decided to save the Toa a trip by stealing it before they could sneak it off.

True, stealing from Toa was only slightly less hazardous than playing blindfolded tag with a catapult scorpion. But with a partner to draw their attention, Hakann was certain he could break in and out before either the Toa or the Frostelus could interfere.

His first mistake had been trusting the Matoran to meet them at the base of the cliff with climbing gear. His second had been hiring Vezok.

"If we get caught, don't worry about getting put in a cage," Vezok growled. "You won't live long enough for that."

Hakann ignored the threat. He was timing the Toa patrolling the ledge. His information was that this blue-green armoured Toa controlled plant life. Hakann smiled, imagining he already smelled the sweet scent of burning shrubbery.

Gritting his sharp teeth, he started to climb again. Vezok followed close behind, grumbling all the way. When they were within arm's length of the edge, Hakann motioned for his partner to stop. Timing was critical now.

The Toa passed right above them. The next instant, Hakann vaulted up onto solid ground and blasted the Toa from behind with his heat vision. Vezok joined in, laughing as he battered the guard with bursts of impact vision. Overcome, the Toa hit the ground.

"Let's throw him over the side," said Vezok, grinning.

"Right. And the second any Toa looks out and sees the sentry missing, alarms go off all over. Honestly, Vezok, I have heard of someone having water in their ears, but never between them."

Hakann hauled the unconscious Toa to his feet and propped him up against a rock. "There. Now he looks like he's just taking a rest. Come on, let's go."

As they ran toward the fortress, Vezok pondered what he had got himself into. Hakann obviously regarded him only as muscle, not realising that Vezok had a reputation as a master thief and a cunning strategist. His gruff voice and overly brutal behaviour were all a cover for a cunning intelligence. His sharp mind told him only one of them was going to make it off this island alive, and Hakann might be surprised to learn which it would be.

Two Toa guarded the rear entrance to the fortress. One carried a mace, and one a flail. Both looked like they could use a bandit or two to break in half, just to relieve the monotony of guard duty.

"Distract them," said Hakann.

"You distract them," Vezok replied. "You're the one in the red armour. They'll see you coming a kio away anyway."

Hakann struggled to control his temper. "Look, how hard does this have to be? Stumble forward, pretend you're hurt, and when they desert their post, I will break in."

"I have a better idea," said Vezok. "Why bother pretending?"

With that, he slammed into Hakann's back, sending the thief flying headlong into the dirt near where the Toa stood. Both reacted immediately, charging toward the intruder with weapons ready. Hakann's only response was a groan of pain.

Vezok took advantage of the opening to rush the door. It was stone and padlocked, but that didn't present a problem. One quick wrench and the lock was snapped. Vezok slipped in and closed the door quietly behind him. Thanks to Hakann's briefing him on the plan, he knew exactly where to look for the treasure.

That had been Hakann's third mistake.

He swiftly made his way through the corridors and up the staircase leading to the tower. More than once, he had to hide in a shadowed doorway to avoid Toa. But having once invaded a cave network filled with thousand-eyed Rahi undetected, this was Matoran's play for him.

A ball of molten lava shot past a tower window. Vezok smiled. Hakann was resisting, just as he had hoped, and drawing more Toa from the base. As long as their attention was focused on their captive, getting away again would be simple.

When he finally broke into the tower room, he was surprised to find it practically bare. The only furniture was a table, upon which rested a stone tablet. Carved into the table were the words *Makoki* stone.

Vezok frowned. This certainly did not look like a treasure. Then again, if he recalled correctly, *Makoki* was the Matoran word for "key."

Is this a key, then? he wondered. *A key to what? Some other vault of treasure? Some secret place? Or was Hakann's information all wrong, and this whole thing is just some joke?*

Angered, Vezok started to knock the stone from the table. Then his keen eyes noticed something strange about it. Although its rough surface looked relatively clean, if one looked close enough, it was possible to see very faint, almost microscopically small scratches upon it. They seemed so random that even if someone spotted them, they would appear to be simply the result of normal wear.

But Vezok was not just anyone. He had a thief's eye for items of true value. He knelt down and peered closely at the stone.

No, those were not random scratches, not at all, he realised. They were a form of writing! It resembled modern Matoran, but was just different enough as to be almost indecipherable. But he could make out enough of it to get a general idea of what was written on the Makoki stone. It was shocking even to him.

This is a record of the Brotherhood of Makuta, he said to himself, keeping even his thoughts to a whisper. *One of the most powerful and benevolent organisations in the universe. Entries on all their members, the locations of their fortresses, everything, all scratched on this stone.*

Vezok knew he should either take it and get going, or else flee empty-handed. But his mind was still trying to process what he had discovered. Why would Toa – self-proclaimed heroes and guardians of justice – be gathering information on another power for good? For what purpose?

The truth slithered into his mind like a

hungry serpent. *The Toa don't trust the Brotherhood,* he realised. *At least, these Toa don't. They are gathering information against the possibility that someday the Brotherhood will betray them.*

This wasn't a treasure. This was an explosive. If the Brotherhood learned of its existence, the Toa would be suspect, or worse, disbanded. And if the Toa found out the stone was gone, they would hunt down the thief to the ends of the universe. Only a fool would risk disaster by stealing such a thing.

A fool, Vezok thought, grabbing the stone, *or someone with dreams of being more than just a simple thief someday.*

Making his way out of the tower, Vezok smiled as he reflected on the name *Makoki.* This stone was a "key" indeed — in fact, he wouldn't be surprised if it did serve as a conventional key to open some lock somewhere. What better way to distract others from its true nature as a key to knowledge, possibly even a key to victory?

He slipped back out the way he had entered. At first, Hakann was nowhere to be seen. Then he spotted a small group of Toa trying to restrain a struggling figure.

Good luck, Hakann, Vezok thought. *By the time you give in and start talking, I will be far away from here.*

As rapidly as he was able, Vezok began scaling the cliff. His boat was lashed to the rocks far below. Once he was safely away, there would be time to decide how best to put this Makoki stone to use.

"Going somewhere?"

The voice came from behind him. Vezok looked over his shoulder, convinced some Toa must have spotted him. But the being he saw was no Toa. He was a powerful figure in blue and gold armour who hovered in midair, arms folded, seeming as casual as if he chatted with other beings on cliffsides every day.

Vezok knew he was at a disadvantage here. If he let go of the cliff to try and fight, he would plunge to his death. Still, he decided it was worth trying to bluff his way through. "I like to rock climb," he sneered. "It's good for my health."

"I know something that isn't," the figure responded. "Stealing from Toa."

"You're an expert on that, are you?" said Vezok.

The figure smiled. "I was robbing Toa back when you were still stealing from Matoran fruit stands. Whatever you found up there, hand it over."

"I didn't find anything," Vezok lied. "Toa don't have anything worth stealing."

"Let me ask that again," the figure responded, firing a Rhotuka spinner from the launcher on his arm. When it struck, Vezok suddenly found it impossible to control his muscles. It seemed as if all his coordination had simply vanished. He lost his grip on the cliff and started to fall, only to be caught in midair by the armoured figure.

"If I have to ask a third time, I'll get

frustrated. When I get frustrated, I drop things."

"All right!" Vezok snapped. "A stone – I found a stone. It's maybe a key to a vault or something, I don't know. I figured I would hold on to it until I discovered what lock it fit."

The figure smiled. "That's better. So you successfully broke into a Toa tower and stole from them, while setting up your partner to be caught? Impressive. I know of someone who might want to meet you...if you are interested in a little dishonest work, that is."

Hanging over a violent sea, kept in the air only by his captor's grip, Vezok would have agreed to cleaning Kikanalo stables by hand. Besides, if he stuck close to this newcomer, maybe he would have the opportunity to steal the stone back.

"Sure," Vezok answered. "But I don't usually go travelling with strangers. What's your name?"

"You can just call me Ancient," the figure

said, gently lowering them both toward the waiting boat. "And as for who I am taking you to meet...he hasn't had a proper name in centuries. We know him as the Shadowed One."

All but one of the Toa in the tower that day met his end at the claws of the Frostelus. The lone survivor, a relatively new and inexperienced master of fire named Lhikan, was ordered by his team leader to flee with the Makoki stone. But when Lhikan went to get the stone, it was gone.

He would search for some years afterward for the tablet, despite the fact that he did not know the true significance of it. Nor did he ever learn just who it was that dared to steal from a Toa tower.

two

When they reached the boat, Ancient explained to Vezok that no outsider was permitted to know the location of the Shadowed One's fortress. Ordinarily, someone being brought for an audience would have their eyes covered in some way to prevent their seeing anything they should not.

"Unfortunately for you, I don't have a blindfold," Ancient said, just before he knocked Vezok unconscious.

The master thief awoke to find himself in a large stone chamber. Although a fire raged in a fireplace, the room was icy cold. The walls were decorated with Kanohi masks, some of them badly damaged. Most striking was what appeared to be a stasis tube in one corner with a Toa inside, trapped in suspended animation.

Vezok did a quick scan of the room, noting exits and how many others stood between him and the way out. Ancient was present, as were four others of Vezok's species, but his attention was drawn to a dark, almost bestial figure sitting on what appeared to be a throne. This, Vezok knew, must be the Shadowed One.

Before anyone could speak, the chamber door opened. An unseen form unceremoniously tossed Hakann inside. The crimson-armoured figure sprawled on the stone floor. Rising, he started to charge for the door, only to be brought up short by the appearance of an ice cage all around him. Heat beams shot from his eyes, but they had no effect on the supercold ice bars.

Noting the expression of surprise on Vezok's face, Hakann snapped, "I escaped!"

"And a wonderful job you're doing of it, too," Vezok muttered in response.

"Be silent, little Piraka," Ancient said. "Listen, that you may hear."

In the moments before the Shadowed One began to speak, Vezok considered the word *Piraka*. In the Matoran language, it meant "thief," among other things, but much more than that as well. A common thief might sneak into a village to steal something of value – a Piraka would set the whole village ablaze to cover up his theft. A robber would normally make an effort to slip in and out unnoticed – a Piraka would destroy whatever or whoever was in sight, purely out of spite.

Piraka were criminals, looked down upon, even by other criminals, as scum. Calling someone by that name was a great way to start a centuries-long feud, usually peppered with violence. There were few words more vile that could come from an intelligent being's mouth.

Strangely, though, Vezok found himself actually liking the term.

He glanced up to see that Ancient had handed the Makoki stone to the Shadowed One. The seated figure examined the tablet for a few moments, then handed it to an aide in bright yellow armour.

"Ambitious," the Shadowed One said, his dark eyes darting from Vezok to Hakann and back. "Tell me, how did you know there was anything worth stealing in that tower?"

Hakann said nothing. Guessing that keeping silent would only lead to a reduction in their life spans, Vezok spoke up. "Hakann got the information from a Matoran."

"Really?" said the Shadowed One, smiling. "What a wise Matoran that must have been."

The chamber door opened again. A tall, thin, winged figure entered, looking confused and hesitant. The Shadowed One beckoned him to come into the chamber.

"This is one of my most effective operatives," the Shadowed One said. He turned to look at Hakann. "But then, I am sure you already know that."

Puzzled by the statement, Vezok glanced at his partner. Hakann was looking at the ceiling, the floor, anywhere but at the newcomer.

Oh, no. He didn't, thought Vezok. If Hakann's "Matoran informer" was a fiction and his true source of information was one of the Shadowed One's agents, things were about to get very, very messy.

"My avian friend here was assigned to steal that very same stone from that very same tower," the Shadowed One continued. "But before he could do so, you two made off with it."

The Shadowed One's expression remained impassive, but his voice hardened. "You see, he was delayed by the time spent selling information to the two of you."

Ancient grabbed the arms of the winged figure before he could move. The Shadowed One rose, eyes crackling with energy.

"You betrayed the Dark Hunters," he said to the struggling prisoner. Then beams of power shot from his eyes. They struck the informer, destroying the bonds of molecular cohesion that kept his body intact. With nothing to hold them together, the unlucky Dark Hunter's atoms shot off in a million different directions, effectively disintegrating him.

"I dislike a traitor," the Shadowed One said, looking directly at his two prisoners. "But I despise an incompetent one. So a word to the wise: If you ever harbor any ideas of betrayal... don't let me catch you."

Vezok nodded, unable to think of anything to say. Hakann didn't even do that.

"I now have a vacancy in my organisation," the Shadowed One went on. "Your lives are about to change, my two thieves...or end."

Hakann, Vezok, and the Shadowed One stood on a terrace overlooking a training arena. The leader of the Dark Hunters had briefly explained his organisation's reason for being. They gained power and profit by doing the jobs others found too dangerous or too illegal to attempt. There were no limits to how far a Dark Hunter would go if the price was right.

"Picture," he said, "beings with the power

and the organisation of the Toa, yet unfettered by their consciences or morality."

Down below, Dark Hunters of various species were engaging in mock combat to hone their skills. The Shadowed One pointed to two trainees in the midst of furious sparring. "The one on the right is called Gladiator. His opponent is a recent recruit named Sidorak. Observe."

The battle that followed was intense, but short. The crimson-armoured Sidorak was powerful, but his fighting style was crude, limited to charging forward in hopes of landing a blow. Gladiator dove, dodged, and showed amazing agility despite his impressive size. When Sidorak, exhausted, gave him an opening, Gladiator struck with two swift blows. Sidorak hit the ground and lay still.

"He's dead?" asked Vezok.

"He wishes he were," the Shadowed One replied.

Other Dark Hunters appeared, to drag Sidorak from the arena like so much trash.

"What happens to him now?" asked Hakann.

"It so happens I may have use for him," said the Shadowed One. "He will be allowed to leave alive, though, of course, our location will be kept concealed from him. If he did not serve some potential purpose, he would be executed and his body returned to his home island as a warning to others."

Hakann watched the failed recruit being taken away and muttered, "Weakling."

"You think so?" asked the Shadowed One. "Good. Because now it's your turn."

With that, he shoved Hakann over the railing. The thief landed with a hard thud on the sand. When Hakann looked up, it was to see a female Dark Hunter smiling down at him and twirling a dagger.

"Get up, Rahi bones," she said with mock sweetness. "Lariska's class is now in session."

Hakann vaulted forward, grabbing a handful of sand as he did so and throwing it in Lariska's eyes. As she staggered back, he used a leg sweep to knock her off her feet.

Once she was down, he took aim with his lava launcher.

Half blind, Lariska hurled a dagger. It struck the launcher, shattering the delicate internal mechanism. With no way now to release the built-up molten energy, the launcher exploded.

When Lariska's vision cleared, she saw Hakann cradling an injured arm. She hurled a dagger right at him. His eyes flashed and beams of heat melted the knife in midair. A second pair of beams lanced toward her. She did a backflip from a standing start, allowing the heat rays to pass beneath her. As soon as her feet hit the ground, she charged, leaped, and executed a perfect flying kick. Slamming into Hakann, she sent him sprawling in the sand.

"Nobody...nobody moves that fast," he said, shaken.

"Oh, I bet you say that to all the females," Lariska answered. "Especially the ones that beat you senseless."

Hakann held up his hand. "I'm a thief, not a warrior. I know when I'm outclassed."

Lariska shrugged and sheathed her dagger.

"And it's not today," Hakann added, as he unleashed a mental blast.

Lariska grabbed her head and reeled. Her very thoughts were now weapons being used against her. She fumbled for a dagger. Hakann increased the power of his blast and drove her to her knees. A few moments more and she pitched forward onto the ground.

Hakann rose and brushed the sand off his armour. It had taken more power than he expected to put Lariska down. But he gathered himself and stood ramrod straight, not wanting to show any sign of weakness. Satisfied that the battle was over, he turned and looked up at the Shadowed One.

"If this is the best you Dark Hunters can offer," he began, "I'll be running this place within a week, and – "

Hakann's remarks were cut off by the feel of a blade at his throat.

"First lesson, Rahi bones," Lariska whispered in his ear. "Don't turn your back on an enemy until you're sure she's stopped breathing. And don't turn your back on a Dark Hunter until her body has rotted in the sun and her armour's been scattered to the winds."

The Shadowed One turned to Vezok. "Decide. Does he live, or does he die?"

Vezok didn't hesitate even for a moment. "Kill him."

The Shadowed One nodded, satisfied. Then he glanced down at Lariska and said, "Let him go. They have both passed their tests."

Reluctantly, Lariska withdrew her knife. Hakann turned and his eyes met hers. There was no respect or regard in his orbs – just pure hatred. "If I were you, I'd keep an eye on those daggers," he said softly. "Or one may wind up in your back someday."

"Don't worry about me," she answered. "I know where all my enemies are. After all, I'm the one who buried them."

Up above, the Shadowed One had summoned Ancient to look after the new recruits and then departed. Vezok watched him go. "How much am I going to regret this?" he wondered aloud.

"Follow orders and do your job, and you will have nothing to regret," Ancient replied. "You'll have food, shelter, protection from your enemies, and the chance to do what you do best: steal, kill, and get away with it. Just one piece of advice..."

Ancient leaned in close, looming over Vezok. "You're going to get your hands on a lot of treasure, everything from jewels to secret knowledge. You'll be tempted to keep some of it and use it for yourself. Don't. The downfall of every Dark Hunter follows the same path, Vezok. First they get greedy...then they get dead."

Hakann and Vezok spent their first night as Dark Hunters sleeping in a rough barracks with a few dozen others. In the morning, they sought out the four other members of their species they had seen in the Shadowed One's chamber.

The first they encountered was Reidak, a brutal sort who was rumored to be a skilled tracker. It wasn't a talent he used often, preferring to simply destroy entire towns until he found the being he was searching for. The Dark Hunters had recruited him after he had done just that, in a fit of temper, to an entire island civilisation.

Two others, Thok and Avak, had similar origins. Both had opposed the Dark Hunters in some way, Avak as a jailer, Thok as a thief who tried to steal from them. Both had talents the Dark Hunters could use, and so they were recruited instead of killed.

Only the last, an emerald-armoured being named Zaktan, proved reluctant to talk with the newcomers. "He doesn't talk much," said Avak. "But there are rumors. Some say he was a slave in a protodermis mine when the

Shadowed One found him. You'd think he would be grateful for being saved from a life like that...but he's constantly being reminded that he used to be a slave and could go back to being one in a heartflash if the Shadowed One willed it."

"There are worse things than slavery, right?" asked Vezok.

"You've obviously never been in a proto mine," Reidak answered. "I don't mean the kind Matoran work in – I mean *real* protodermis mines, where it's not just a job, it's a death sentence."

Vezok eyed Zaktan carefully. He had seen more than his share of dangerous beings, but something about Zaktan gave him a chill. It was as if someone had taken rage and evil and given those qualities a body to walk around in.

One day, he's going to do something beyond what we can imagine, Vezok thought. Maybe replace the Shadowed One...maybe get his hands on something that will make the Toa and the Brotherhood bow down to him...or maybe just lead us into the fire and destroy us all.

three

Five Thousand Years Ago...

"In or out?" asked Zaktan. "Decide."

Vezok looked around the small chamber. It was cramped and damp and smelled of dead Rahi. If greed and ambition had scents, it would have reeked of those, too.

Hakann, Thok, and Reidak were standing in the back of the room, their eyes locked onto Vezok. Only Avak was missing, deemed too untrustworthy to be included in this conversation.

"If I go in with you?" answered Vezok.

"Then we strike tonight. By morning, the Shadowed One will be a memory, his allies will be in chains, and we will be running the Dark Hunters." When Zaktan put it that way, it sounded easy – so easy that it made Vezok even more nervous.

"And if I'm out?"

Reidak bared his teeth in a wolfish grin that left no doubt Vezok would not be leaving the chamber under his own power if he gave the wrong answer.

"We have the numbers?" asked Vezok.

Zaktan nodded. "Enough so that we really don't need you. We are only making the offer out of...species loyalty, so to speak. Discontent with the Shadowed One's rule has been spreading among the Dark Hunters for years. Wander the island and try and find someone who doesn't resent handing over every treasure they find, or who hasn't been imprisoned – or worse – for offending our leader. The Shadowed One is ripe for overthrow."

"His spies – "

"Are known," Hakann finished. "And will be dealt with, when the time comes."

Vezok snarled, angry at himself for having such a hard time with this decision. After all, he owed the Shadowed One no loyalty. He had never wanted to be part of this organisation in the first place. He had been perfectly happy as an independent thief. He was free to live the way he pleased. Now it was looking like just staying alive might be a challenge.

"All right," he said. "I'm in."

At any given time, there were anywhere from fifty to a hundred Dark Hunters based on the Shadowed One's island. Some were there for rest and recreation between missions, others for training, and a few the Dark Hunter's leader just wanted to keep where he could see them. Zaktan's plan hinged on the theory that most of the island's inhabitants were either sick of the Shadowed One's rule or really didn't care who was in charge.

The five conspirators split up after their meeting and spent the rest of the day trying to remain inconspicuous. Zaktan had suggested they approach the Shadowed One's fortress in pairs, coming from different directions and at slightly different times. Two Dark Hunters reporting in was not unusual, but five showing up at once would seem suspicious.

There were only a small number of guards on duty at the fortress gates, led by a bizarre figure nicknamed Prototype. He was the product of a forced merge between a Toa of Fire and a Toa of Earth, which somehow resulted in a hybrid entity possessing enormous power, very little sanity, and really big claws. Still, it wasn't Prototype or the guards he could see that worried Vezok – it was the ones he couldn't see that would be the problem.

As discussed, Vezok approached Prototype and struck up a conversation to give Zaktan the chance to ambush him. This was not an easy task, since Prototype was not much of a conversationalist. Still, Vezok succeeded in getting him to turn his back to Zaktan.

Zaktan glanced around, made sure no one was looking, and fired a blast of his laser vision at Prototype. To his shock, the beams just bounced off harmlessly. Prototype noticed the attack, though, for he turned to Zaktan and said, "Not nice." Then he batted his attacker away.

"Stupid," Prototype said, shaking his head. "Bright lights don't bother me. Nothing bothers me."

Vezok's first instinct was to attack and try to knock Prototype out. Then he remembered the sight of the half-conscious Zaktan flying through the air. "You're right," Vezok said. "He is stupid. In fact, I think he's a traitor to the Dark Hunters."

"He is?"

"Yes," Vezok answered. "You need to go tell the Shadowed One about this now. He's in the training facility on the far side of the island."

"But I thought he was inside?"

"Do you think the Shadowed One is going

to stop and tell you every place he's going?" Vezok asked harshly. "Now get going! If Zaktan hurts anyone because you didn't give a warning, you know who will get blamed."

It took Prototype a solid minute to realise the answer was him. Then he shrugged and lumbered away in search of the Shadowed One. *With luck*, Vezok thought, *it will be a while before he remembers there is no training facility on the far side of the island.*

By then, Zaktan had staggered back, looking for the massive guard. His rage only grew when he couldn't find Prototype. "Where is he?" he seethed.

"Gone," Vezok answered. "I did what you should have done in the first place. We needed him away from the gate, Zaktan, that's all. We don't need to start a war."

Zaktan eyed Vezok warily. "And if there were a war, are you quite sure whose side you would be on?"

"The same side I'm always on," Vezok replied, opening the iron gate. "My own."

A few minutes later, they were joined by Hakann, followed by Thok and Reidak. They reported that no one on the island seemed to suspect that anything strange was going on. Those Dark Hunters most loyal to the Shadowed One had been summoned by Hakann to a secret meeting to discuss security concerns. Once they were all assembled, he had slipped out and informed a half dozen of the more powerful guards that a group of traitors was conspiring against the Shadowed One. He pointed them to the chamber where the loyalists were meeting and insisted that no one inside should be allowed to leave under any circumstances. The Shadowed One would be coming personally to see to their arrest and punishment.

"Very well," whispered Zaktan. "We will head to the central chamber and take the Shadowed One and any of his lieutenants who may be present. Then the island will be ours."

"Hold it!" said Vezok. "Where are all the rest? I thought you said you had the numbers to do this."

"We do," answered Hakann. "Five is a very good number. Of course, four has its appeal, too...."

"Power divided in too many ways is no longer worth having," said Zaktan. "It would be as if your body were to be split into a million pieces, each capable of acting independently. You would be formidable...but never again whole."

Zaktan beckoned the others to follow him. It was only a short journey through the dank corridors to reach the central chamber. Down one hallway, turn right, down another, turn left, and...

They were facing a blank stone wall. It hadn't been there the day before. Instead, there had been a long corridor leading directly to the Shadowed One's chamber.

"We...we must have made a wrong turn," said Hakann nervously.

The party went back the way they had come. But they could not retrace their steps exactly, for another blank wall had appeared where a hallway had been moments before. They were forced to turn right instead of left, then keep turning left as they followed a new path along the inside edge of the fortress. Every time it seemed they must be coming close to an exit, another wall would block their way.

"We're going in a circle!" Reidak snapped. "What are you up to, Zaktan?"

"It's not my doing!" Zaktan replied, his voice ragged. "It's this place. Nothing is like it was yesterday!"

"Not even you."

The voice came from up above. The five Dark Hunters looked up to see one of the most dreaded figures on the island, the stalker in the shadows, called Darkness. His traditional place of residence was among the stone beams of the ceiling above the Shadowed One's throne. If the Dark Hunter leader showed the slightest sign of weakness, remorse, or compassion, it would be Darkness's job to slay him so that another could take his place. He left the chamber only rarely, to "sharpen his claws" by disciplining disobedient members of the organisation. His presence here and now represented nothing short of total disaster.

"Then the Shadowed One knows...?" asked Zaktan. It was the first time Vezok had ever heard fear in his voice.

Darkness nodded once.

"We have to get out of here!" Hakann yelled, already running in what he thought was the direction of the exit. Reidak and Thok followed him, but Vezok paused for a moment.

"You know what will happen to us," he said to Zaktan. "Why aren't you fleeing?"

"This is an island. Where would I run?" Zaktan replied. "Where could I go where he will not find me?"

Vezok knew he was right. The Dark

Hunters had a long reach. There was nowhere in the known universe to conceal yourself from them. But he ran anyway, because that is what one does when destruction is drawing near.

None of them got very far, of course. The appearance of new walls effectively herded them into the central chamber where the Shadowed One, Darkness, Ancient, and the yellow-armoured figure called Sentrakh waited.

Vezok expected the Shadowed One to lash out at them, accuse them of being traitors, and threaten them with all sorts of horrible punishments. But he said nothing. He simply sat on his throne and stared at each one of them in turn. Vezok had thought there might be disappointment or rage in his eyes, but they were flat and dead. Somehow, that seemed much worse than if he had been in a fury.

Finally, he beckoned Zaktan to step

forward. The Shadowed One exhaled, smiled, and visibly relaxed. For a moment, Vezok thought that maybe they might be ok.

Then the Shadowed One's eyes turned crimson. Twin beams of power lanced out and struck Zaktan. There was a blinding flash of light.

When it faded, Zaktan still stood there, but he had changed in a terrible way. He was standing still, but his body was moving, as if each individual cell had taken on a life of its own. Panicked, Zaktan lost control and his mass began to dissipate. Like a swarm of fireflies broken up by a windstorm, fragments of Zaktan began to drift away. It was the most terrible thing Vezok had ever seen, in a lifetime filled with many awful sights.

He looked at the Shadowed One and was surprised to see that the Dark Hunter leader looked stunned as well. Apparently, this was not the effect the beams were supposed to have had. Something had gone very wrong.

Zaktan suddenly calmed down. Exerting a

force of will Vezok never imagined any being had, he drew the disconnected parts of himself back together. He was whole again, or at least as whole as any being in his condition could be.

The Shadowed One, too, had regained his composure. He settled back in his chair and gazed around at the assembled conspirators. "Remember," he said, in the soft tone of a doom viper's hiss.

Zaktan would eventually discover that his body had been converted to billions of microscopic protodites. Each contained a portion of his consciousness and could function independently of his body as a whole. This allowed him to send parts of himself on the attack as a swarm, to fly, to evade physical attacks more easily, and to slip through spaces too small for even an insect.

He never spoke about what happened to him that night, nor did he ever allow anyone else to speak of it. He learned to adapt to his new condition and harness the powers it gave him. Eventually, he became a hundred times more effective as a Dark Hunter than he had ever been before.

And he never, not even for a moment, stopped hating the Shadowed One.

four

Four Thousand Years Ago...

"Everyone who thinks this is a bad idea," grumbled Reidak, "scream at the top of your lungs."

"Shut up and steer," said Vezok. "Do you want all of Metru Nui to hear us coming?"

The two Dark Hunters, along with a third, Avak, were in a small skiff sailing through the sea gate toward the island city of Metru Nui. It was a risky trip. Turaga Dume, the city's leader, had forbidden Dark Hunters to enter the area years before. His stated reasons were that they brought lawlessness and violence with them, but the truth was that he knew the Shadowed One had his eyes on Metru Nui. He was not going to allow them to get a foothold on the island and then attempt to overthrow him.

His problem was enforcing this law. Metru Nui had no Toa. It was one of the safest places in the universe, because everyone knew how vital the city was to the well-being of so many other lands. The goods it traded were desperately needed elsewhere and the energy produced by the power plants was so great it could be funneled to other cities at no cost to Metru Nui. Destroying the island and its inhabitants would be an act of madness. Therefore there had never been a need for the Toa to maintain a presence in the city.

However, no one had considered the possibility of attempting to conquer the city. Until now.

"Are we there yet?" asked Avak. He was in the centre of the boat, rowing lazily. Every now and again, he would amuse himself by mentally creating a prison around some sea bird and watching it flutter about, trying to escape.

"If our information is right, the sea cave should be just below," Vezok replied. He looked around at where their journey had brought them. Metru Nui was surrounded by a huge silver sea, bounded on all four sides by massive rock walls. Portals were carved in some of these walls to allow for boats to pass through on their way to and from the city.

Reidak peered over the side of the boat at the silvery water. Large aquatic Rahi could dimly be seen swimming far below. Somehow, he doubted they were all vegetarians. "So who's going down there?" he asked.

"I thought we all would," Vezok answered. "It may take three of us to – "

"Someone has to guard the boat, and I volunteer," Avak broke in, talking so fast one word blurred into the next.

"I volunteer to guard Avak guarding the boat and make sure he doesn't leave without us," Reidak offered.

Vezok frowned. "You heard the Shadowed One. You know what's supposed to be down there. If I go down alone, I'll end up a light snack. So who's going to help me?"

Avak looked at Reidak and said, "I'll flip you for it." When Reidak nodded agreement, Avak lunged forward, grabbed him, and flipped him over the side of the boat and into the water. "Looks like I win."

Reidak's response was a string of curses that could have seared the scales off a stone serpent. Vezok chuckled and plunged into the water as well. "Stay with the boat," he said to Avak. Then he added, "And the boat stays *here*."

Vezok and Reidak dove beneath the surface. The water was icy cold, worse than the snowcapped peaks of the Dark Hunter island. Their armour made it difficult to maneuver underwater, but if they had to rely on their agility, they were doomed anyway. Strength would be the difference down here.

Reidak's eyes flared red. His infrared vision pierced the dark water, but revealed only the heat of passing Rahi fish. He would have to do this the hard way, by searching and hoping the Shadowed One's information was accurate. Both he and Vezok knew there was no time to waste – even their oversize lungs could hold only so much air.

When they were close to the sea bottom,

Reidak stopped and pointed. Vezok saw a massive boulder ringed with ice, apparently serving to block the entrance of a sea cave. The two Dark Hunters struck as one, smashing the rock to rubble. Beyond it was a solid block of ice at least a hundred feet thick.

Vezok nodded. The legend was accurate, then. He wished that Hakann was with them to use his heat vision on the ice. Then he realised that "I wish Hakann was here" were words he had never expected to say, and would probably never say again.

Reidak started to pound on the ice. Vezok blasted the block with his impact vision. Periodically, they had to surface to get some air. Then they would dive down again and resume their work.

After more than two hours, the last fragment of ice fell away to reveal the "treasure" inside. Vezok saw a great red eye flicker open, followed by another. The temperature of the water suddenly shot up, almost to the boiling point. A low rumble in the water grew into a great bellow. Inside the cave, something began to crawl toward freedom.

Eyes wide with panic, Vezok gestured upward. Reidak got the idea and the two of them shot for the surface. They scrambled aboard the boat even as Avak said, "What? What is it? What did you see?"

"Row! Row!" Vezok yelled. "Get us out of here!"

Avak complied, but not before he turned to see if he could spot the source of their disturbance. Something was moving underwater, getting closer, closing in fast. Suddenly it burst up from below, capsizing the boat and sending all three Dark Hunters into the water. Then it dove beneath the waves again.

"What was that?" Avak shouted.

"A little present," Vezok answered. "From the Shadowed One to Metru Nui, with best wishes."

* * *

The great beast swam free for the first time in thousands of years. It had only dim memories of its past, but what had gone before didn't matter to it at the moment. The only thing the Kanohi Dragon cared about was that it was very, very hungry.

Sensing a tremendous source of heat on the island up ahead, it moved in that direction. Heat meant life, and life meant food, and today he would at last eat well.

"So we found him," said Reidak. The three were back in their boat again. "Now do we go home?"

"No," said Vezok. "Now we wait."

"For what?"

"For what's bound to happen."

The Kanohi Dragon's massive tail slashed through the water. It was closer to the heat, but there was still a great distance to cover. Now it remembered this place and the little ones who lived in it. The dragon had been here before, long before so many buildings had crowded together on the island. It had come to feed then, too, but the inhabitants had caused it pain. Flying over the city would just invite them to do it again.

Then it would not fly, it decided. Although the cold water was uncomfortable and swimming not its favored means of transport, it would stay under the water. It would find a way to the heat without the little ones noticing. Then, when its strength had returned, old scores would be settled.

"They don't stand a chance," said Avak. "The city will be a ruin by tomorrow."

"No, it won't," Reidak answered, smiling. "Because we're going to save it, aren't we, Vezok?"

Vezok decided he had better rethink just how smart Reidak actually was. The Shadowed One had shared the complete plan only with him, but Reidak had managed to figure it all out. *I will have to watch him,* thought Vezok. *He's not what he seems.*

"A few hours with the Kanohi Dragon on a rampage should convince Turaga Dume that his city needs protection," Vezok said. "With no Toa in sight, the Dark Hunters will generously agree to 'protect' it in return for locating a base here. It's a good plan."

"Sure," Avak said, nodding. "Only how are we supposed to stop that thing, if they agree?"

Vezok started rowing toward the city. "I said it was a good plan. I didn't say it was a perfect plan."

The Kanohi Dragon smashed through an intricate series of suboceanic chutes, then battered its way through the thick walls of the Metru Nui Archives. Matoran scrambled down to investigate the source of the terrible crash and flooding. As soon as they saw the monstrous Rahi that had broken in, they scrambled back up again as fast as their legs could carry them.

The dragon didn't care anything about them, not yet. Its goal was the source of heat, which was still some distance away. Rather than go aboveground, it made its way through the lowest levels of the Archives.

A daring Onu-Matoran archivist named Mavrah took a chance and followed. The creature's path was littered with smashed cylinders, crushed artifacts, and sundered walls. More than a few living "exhibits" had been freed, forcing Mavrah to move with caution in case any of them were hungry. It rapidly became clear that the monster was not moving at random, but rather in a straight line toward Ta-Metru.

Mavrah would have pursued the dragon all the way to the Great Furnace if his friend Whenua had not caught up to him and made him stop. He was followed closely by the Chief Archivist, whose mask concealed the grief he felt at the sight of such destruction.

"Turaga Dume has called out the Vahki," Whenua said, referring to the mechanized security forces of Metru Nui. "But I'm not sure even they can handle this."

"It's...amazing," Mavrah whispered in awe. "I've never seen a Rahi like it. Why is it here? What does it want? There's so much we could learn!"

"You can study its corpse," the Chief Archivist snapped. "Now come away from here. We must return to the upper levels."

The three Matoran turned away, trying to ignore the sounds of battle already filling the Archives.

Vezok, Reidak, and Avak landed the boat on a secluded part of the Le-Metru coastline. Vezok pointed to the squads of Vahki soaring toward Ta-Metru. "I guess they figured out something's wrong. Well, we'll wait until dark. Let them sweat a little."

Avak was looking around for some way to amuse himself until nightfall when he spotted a dozen Vahki heading in their direction. He was bracing for battle when they flew by overhead, travelling out over the ocean and away from the city.

Now where are they going? he wondered.

* * *

The Vahki proved to be no more than an annoyance for the Kanohi Dragon. The heat generated by the now fully thawed creature melted most of the city's guardians. The rest fell to its claws and teeth. It moved unopposed to the area just below Ta-Metru. Once it was beneath the source of greatest heat, it smashed its way through the ceiling.

The dragon found itself in the heart of the Great Furnace. Matoran scattered in panic as it plunged into the flames.

As darkness fell on Metru Nui, it was a city in fear. Fires had spread out of control in Ta-Metru. The streets were littered with pieces of the mechanical Vahki. Matoran were gathering weapons and preparing to make a futile attack on the dragon.

Turaga Dume sat in his chamber in the

Coliseum, brooding on the fate of his city. A slight shift in the atmosphere of the room told him he was no longer alone.

"Having a bad day?" asked Vezok.

Dume looked up at the three Dark Hunters who had invaded his sanctum. A lesser being would have fled at the sight. But Dume had been a Toa and later a Turaga for centuries. His heart knew no fear.

"I should have guessed," he said, rising. "The Kanohi Dragon is the weapon, but the hand that wields it belongs to the Shadowed One."

"It's a real shame what's happening out there," said Reidak. "It sure would be awful if the Kanohi Dragon trashed Ta-Metru. Would be even worse if something like this happened every week."

"It should be obvious the Vahki can't protect you," Vezok added. "Work with us, and you won't have to worry about this sort of thing anymore."

A cold silence descended on the room. Dume turned his back on the Dark Hunters, deep in thought. The seconds dragged by. Then the leader of Metru Nui spoke once more.

"Get out."

"You're making a mistake," Avak snarled. "A *big* mistake."

Dume ignored him and locked eyes with Vezok. "I'll see this city reduced to rubble... with not even two bricks still together...before

I'll let your kind take root here."

"Now you're not thinking about the best interests of your city," Vezok replied. He raised his harpoon weapon and aimed it at Dume. "Maybe it's time Metru Nui had new leadership."

Vezok triggered his weapon even as a bolt of flame flew into the room. Fire met harpoon halfway across the chamber and melted the projectile. The Dark Hunters turned to see two Toa — one emerald in colour, one red and gold — standing in the window. Nine other Toa hovered on Vahki in the night sky behind them.

"Toa Lhikan!" exclaimed Dume. "Toa Nidhiki!"

"You didn't tell us you had Dark Hunters visiting," said Nidhiki, Toa of Air. "Here I thought we would be fighting only higher forms of life."

"We got your message," said Toa Lhikan, master of fire. "Are these three responsible for the trouble here?"

Dume hesitated. He would have dearly loved to see these three Dark Hunters imprisoned, but doing so would just lead to more being sent to free them. Metru Nui would become a battleground. A more diplomatic solution was needed.

"They are couriers for a different message from me," the Turaga replied. "They were just leaving to go back to their home."

The look in Lhikan's eyes told Dume the Toa understood exactly what was going on here. "Probably wise," Lhikan said. Then, looking right at the Dark Hunters, he added, "It's not safe here."

Vezok got the hint. He and the others would take on two Toa and a Turaga any day. But eleven Toa was another matter entirely. There was nothing to be gained by such a fight, and way too much that could be lost.

"So it seems," he said to Lhikan. "But it's a beautiful city. Maybe, when things have calmed down, we'll come back."

"I'll be happy to show you around," said

Toa Nidhiki, smiling. "You can get a great view of the whole place from atop the Knowledge Towers...as long as you don't slip and fall off."

Vezok returned the Toa's smile, but both knew it was more a mutual challenge than anything else. Then he led Reidak and Avak out of the Coliseum. Once outside, Toa kept a watchful eye on them until they were in their boat and away.

"Well, that went well," grumbled Reidak.

Vezok shrugged. "It's not over. It may take a year, a century, or a few thousand years...but the Shadowed One gets what he wants."

Lhikan, Nidhiki, and their team of Toa waged a month-long battle with the Kanohi Dragon. Scores of buildings were destroyed, entire sections of Ta-Metru were rendered uninhabitable, and far too many innocent Matoran met their deaths. When the beast was finally defeated (thanks in no small part to the combined efforts of four Toa of Ice), it was not a victory that filled the Toa's hearts with pride, just relief.

While the fate of the dragon was being debated, Nidhiki took it upon himself to try and kill it. But the armoured scales that had deflected so many blows during the fight prevented him from ending the creature's life. It was finally decided to transport the dragon to another island whose rulers had agreed to give it refuge and keep it away from other lands. Lhikan and a half dozen of his team agreed to man the barge carrying the dragon, while Nidhiki and the rest stayed behind to secure the city.

"The Dark Hunters won't take no for an answer," Lhikan reminded Dume. "They'll be back. So will we."

It was a journey of many days to the Kanohi Dragon's new home. Once there, the barge sailed up to a dock made of black, twisted metal. The look and feel of the island disturbed the Toa. Though parts seemed tropical and wild, much of the rest of it was covered with dull iron buildings that spewed foul smoke into the sky. One of the team insisted he had seen factory doors open and what looked like an array of war machines assembled inside.

A tall, ebon being approached the Toa. Dark eyes darted from the heroes to the Kanohi Dragon. A vicious mouth curved into a smile.

"This will do," the figure hissed. "This will do very nicely."

"I am Toa Lhikan. We sailed from Metru Nui to bring this creature here, but I must ask you: Are you sure you want such an evil, dangerous beast on your island?"

"Evil is all relative, Toa of Fire," the smiling figure replied. "In your city, this is a monster. On my island, it is...an ill-tempered pet. So, the answer is yes. Speaking for my home, I, Roodaka, welcome the Kanohi Dragon to our shores."

five

Three Thousand Years Ago...

Hakann crouched on a Ga-Metru rooftop. Lariska was next to him, toying with her blades as she always did. At first, Hakann had dismissed this as a nervous habit. Later, he realised her daggers were probably the only "friends" she truly trusted.

It was another dark, cold, and dangerous night in Metru Nui. Hakann had seen too many of them by now. After the incident with the Kanohi Dragon, the Shadowed One had made a few more attempts – some obvious, some not – to either seize control of the city or else secure a base there. Each time, his efforts had been frustrated by the Toa.

It came as no surprise that the Shadowed One had become obsessed with Metru Nui.

When an attempt by Thok to kidnap Turaga Dume failed, the ruler of the Dark Hunters reached the end of his patience. He assembled a legion of his best operatives and ordered them to invade and capture Metru Nui. This struck many, including Hakann, as a very strange and highly risky idea. Dark Hunters lived in the shadows, struck quickly, and disappeared. They didn't form armies and invade cities.

"There's a word for a Dark Hunter in daylight," Hakann had said at the time. "A target."

Still, the plan had seemed to be working. A couple of hundred Dark Hunters stormed Metru Nui in the dead of night, taking the Vahki and Lhikan's team of Toa completely by surprise. While the Matoran took cover, they seized control of most of the city. The Toa and Turaga Dume were forced to take refuge inside the Coliseum. Victory seemed only days away.

Then everything went wrong. The Toa of

Water managed to slip through the Dark Hunter lines and swim the ocean. At the first island she came to, she dragged herself to the Turaga and begged for help for Metru Nui. The result was that close to one hundred Toa descended on the city and turned what should have been a quick fight into a protracted siege. Toa and Dark Hunters clashed in metru-to-metru, street-to-street fighting that lasted months.

By now, both sides were hurting badly. Work in the city had largely ground to a halt. Damage to the different metru was extensive. Meanwhile, with so many Dark Hunters tied down in Metru Nui, the flow of treasure coming into the vaults of the organisation had slowed to a trickle. Both Dume and the Shadowed One knew some bold stroke was needed to end this war before there was nothing left to fight over.

Hakann's recollections were interrupted by the sight of a lone Toa on the streets below. It was a Toa of Air, judging from the colour of his armour, and his mask and weapon matched Vezok's description of Toa Nidhiki. Hakann smiled. Here was a wonderful opportunity to not only take one more Toa out of the fight, but rob Vezok of a chance for revenge at the same time.

He was about to spring when Lariska stopped him. "One more dead Toa does us no good," she said. "Let me handle this."

"And grab more glory for yourself?" Hakann snarled.

Lariska smiled in reply. "Let me put this another way. Stay out of my way while I handle this or we'll pick up where we left off in the Shadowed One's arena."

Without another word, she leapt to another rooftop, then another, and finally to the ground. She was moving in the general direction of the Coliseum, a sure way to attract the attention of a Toa.

Down below, Nidhiki took the bait. There was a brief, inconclusive fight that left Hakann unsatisfied. There had been at least three perfect openings for Lariska to kill the Toa and she had let all of them slip by. He wondered if there might be some way to use that information to his advantage.

The Toa disappeared briefly. Hakann could hear Lariska talking. Then Nidhiki was visible again and he and Lariska were having a discussion. Hakann was too far away to hear what they were saying. He considered and rejected the idea of Lariska planning to defect to the Toa. *She'd look lousy in a mask and she knows it,* he thought.

When Lariska returned, she had a look on her face like a Muaka who had just eaten a Gukko bird. "He's willing to deal. We have to get a message to the Shadowed One."

"What if it's a trick?"

Lariska shook her head. "I don't think so. He's nowhere near as a good a liar as he thinks he is. Someday, that will probably cost him."

The message dispatched via trained Nui-Rama was short and to the point. Toa Nidhiki would arrange for the capture of Turaga Dume, Toa Lhikan, and the rest of Metru Nui's defenders in exchange for rule over the city. The Shadowed One's answer was just as direct: Agree to Nidhiki's demands, and once the war was won, eliminate him.

Lariska had arranged a meeting with Nidhiki for the next night. As before, Hakann remained in the shadows and watched. He knew better than to trust a Toa, and he wasn't completely certain of Lariska's motives, either. Maybe she was planning to cut herself in as future queen of Metru Nui.

Nidhiki was late and looked worried. "What's the answer? Come on, come on, I'm risking everything just being here!"

"Calm down," said Lariska. "Were you followed here?"

"I don't think so," said Nidhiki. "Lhikan told me to head down to the docks to meet a supply boat. He can't tear himself away from being leader of the Toa army long enough to actually do any work."

He's bitter, thought Hakann. *Ok, we can work with that.*

"It's a deal," Lariska said. "Tomorrow you lead Lhikan and the Coliseum guard into the Canyon of Unending Whispers in Po-Metru. We'll be scattered in the caves and foothills. Once it's over, I'm to take care of Turaga Dume personally...and the city will be yours, Nidhiki. What do you plan to do with it?"

Hakann didn't hear Nidhiki's answer. His attention was drawn to a brief gleam of red and gold from a nearby rooftop. It was Toa Lhikan! He had followed Nidhiki and heard everything.

The Dark Hunter's mind raced. If he warned Lariska, the "trap" could be called off in plenty of time to save the Shadowed One's army. On the other hand, if he didn't, Lariska would be disgraced and the war would be over. The only flaw would be, he would wind up a prisoner of the Toa. He needed to find a way to save his own metallic hide.

Nidhiki left. Lariska had not yet returned.

Hakann climbed up to the roof and began following Toa Lhikan.

It didn't take long for the Toa to detect his presence. Lhikan whirled and hurled flames from his two fire greatswords. Hakann evaded and hit Lhikan with a mental blast. The Toa staggered, but recovered, slamming his two swords together to make a shield. He then tossed the shield with incredible accuracy, knocking Hakann's feet out from under him. The shield was on its way back to Lhikan when Hakann nailed it with his heat vision, sending it spiraling off course. The Dark Hunter sprang to his feet, lava launcher pointed right at Toa Lhikan.

"I could kill you now, Toa, but there's been enough killing," Hakann said, making an effort to sound sincerely concerned about the loss of life. In truth, the only life he cared anything for was his own. "It's time to end this war."

Lhikan said nothing, simply glared at Hakann with contempt. He might as well have thrown a snowball for all his opinion mattered to the Dark Hunter.

"You know what your pal Nidhiki is planning with us. You're probably setting up a trap of your own," said Hakann. "You figure you'll slap all of us into a prison cave somewhere until the stars go out. But...maybe there's a deal to be made here."

"I don't make deals with Dark Hunters," Lhikan snapped.

"You'll deal with this one," Hakann replied, doing his best to control his temper. "Or maybe you'd rather not know what happened to the Makoki stone, all those years ago?"

Lhikan's body language conveyed, if only for a moment, that he was surprised by Hakann's statement. Sensing an opening, the Dark Hunter pressed on.

"I stole it," he lied. "And I gave it to the Shadowed One as a sort of entrance fee into the Dark Hunters. If we are going to lose this war, then we are — but I propose a trade. You get the Makoki stone, and we leave this island under our power."

Toa Lhikan wrestled with the idea. Free, the Dark Hunters would always be a threat. But the Makoki stone was something his fellow Toa had been willing to die to protect thousands of years before. Even if he didn't know its true importance, it must have been vital in some way. Could he betray the memory of his deceased comrades by passing up the chance to get it back?

"You'll come with me," Lhikan said. "Then you'll send a message to your leader. Tell him the war is lost. If he hands over the Makoki stone, we'll let you and the other Dark Hunters leave Metru Nui and return home...on two conditions."

"Which are?"

"You never come back...ever...and you take Nidhiki with you. I want him out of my sight."

Hakann smiled. "How do I know you'll keep your end of the deal?"

"Toa don't go back on their word," Lhikan replied.

Hakann chuckled. "I guess Nidhiki must

have missed that part of the training."

Everything went as Toa Lhikan had planned it. When he, Nidhiki, and the rest of the Coliseum guard marched into the Canyon of Unending Whispers, they were immediately ambushed by Dark Hunters. A moment later, the Dark Hunters found themselves surrounded by three hundred Toa who had arrived in the city on the "supply boats" the night before.

Having lived under the harsh discipline of the Shadowed One for so long, the Dark Hunters fully expected the same treatment from the Toa. Failure, they assumed, would mean death.

"Now what?" a defiant Lariska asked Toa Lhikan. "Do you march us all into the sea?"

Hakann held his breath. Would Lhikan keep his part of the bargain?

The Toa of Fire hesitated a moment. Then he said, "A messenger was sent to the Shadowed One before you ever reached the canyon. You will be allowed to walk out of here the same way you walked in."

Lhikan went on to outline the same conditions he had related to Hakann. Nidhiki was shocked to discover that he, too, was being banished from the city. Lariska looked disappointed – death would have been preferable to the punishment the Shadowed One would dish out for her failure. The entire scene filled Hakann with glee.

By the next morning, the Dark Hunters and Nidhiki had been loaded into ships headed for the Shadowed One's island. Nidhiki stood by himself at the rail, gazing at the city he was sure he would never see again. None of the Dark Hunters came anywhere near him. Watching the scene, Hakann could not help but remember the Shadowed One's words from so long ago – "I dislike a traitor. But I despise an incompetent one."

The Shadowed One would keep his word,

as much as he ever did. It would be 2,000 years before another Dark Hunter would set foot on Metru Nui – and one of the three who would make the return trip would be Nidhiki.

The ruler of the Dark Hunters was not, however, content to allow the Makoki stone to remain in Toa hands. Six months after the

Dark Hunter surrender on Metru Nui, he dispatched a team to the Toa base where the stone was being held. They successfully stole the tablet. The Shadowed One ordered it split into six pieces so he could earn six times the ransom for it. The Brotherhood of Makuta were the high bidders for the stones, despite the fact that they, too, had no idea of their true significance.

The only other problem left over from the Toa – Dark Hunter war was Nidhiki himself. Despite Lariska's insistence that neither she nor the ex-Toa were responsible for the defeat, she was punished severely and Nidhiki was shunned. The Shadowed One valued Nidhiki's knowledge and experience but could not bring himself to fully trust him. He knew also that Nidhiki was scheming to escape the island in hopes of someday resuming his career as a Toa.

The Shadowed One's solution to this situation was elegantly evil. He allowed Nidhiki to get so close to freedom the ex-Toa could practically taste it. Then, at the last moment, he had a new recruit, Roodaka, use her powers to mutate Nidhiki into an insectoid monster. Now so hideous that Matoran society would never accept him, he was doomed to remain a Dark Hunter for the rest of his days.

And how about the rest of us? Hakann wondered, as he watched Nidhiki react in horror to his new form. *Are we all to stay Dark Hunters forever? Or will there be an opportunity someday to say good-bye to this wretched place...and have power the Shadowed One never even dreamed of?*

It was an idea well worth thinking about, he decided.

SIX

Two Hundred Fifty Years Ago...

Reidak was a happy Dark Hunter.

He had been posted to the south wall of a Dark Hunter fortress for the last day and a half. His orders were simple: anyone or anything that tried to get over the wall was to be crushed, stomped, flattened, and otherwise discouraged from trying it again. So far, he had gotten to practice his favourite hobby – destruction – on a squad of Rahkshi, one suit of Exo-Toa armour running on automatic, and a dozen Rahi wearing infected Kanohi masks that controlled their actions. The forces of the Brotherhood of Makuta were sure to mount another attack soon, which was fine with him. Reidak hoped this joy would never end.

Relations between the Brotherhood and the Dark Hunters had been souring for some time. It had been Dark Hunters who were on guard when six Toa, the Toa Hagah, succeeded in stealing both the Makoki stones and the Kanohi Mask of Light from the Brotherhood. Although the Dark Hunters on duty had fought hard and well, they were still blamed for allowing the thefts to happen. The Brotherhood had insisted on the execution of the guards involved, but the Shadowed One had refused. The matter ended there...or it seemed to, anyway.

Three centuries later, the Makuta of Metru Nui hired three Dark Hunters – Nidhiki, a dumb brute named Krekka, and a third, codenamed Eliminator – to aid him in a takeover of Metru Nui. The effort failed. In a desperate bid to restore lost energies quickly, Makuta absorbed both Nidhiki and Krekka into his own substance, killing them. Eliminator knew nothing of this, and neither did any other Dark Hunter. All they knew was that Nidhiki and Krekka never returned from their mission.

A short time later, the discovery of the Kanohi Vahi, the Mask of Time, had drawn both the Shadowed One and the Makuta of Metru Nui to that city. They came into conflict over possession of the mask. The revelation that Makuta had slain two Dark Hunters turned the argument into a battle. Although severely wounded, Makuta managed to defeat the leader of the Dark Hunters. The prize eluded them both, however, thanks to the quick thinking of a Toa of Fire named Vakama.

Still, the damage had been done. The Shadowed One vowed revenge and declared war on the Brotherhood of Makuta. To most members of the organisation, this seemed like declaring war on the sun or the sea. The power wielded by the Brotherhood was unimaginable. The accepted wisdom was that the Dark Hunters would be crushed within a matter of weeks.

That had not proved to be the case. The Brotherhood had their hands full dealing with the after-effects of a bioquake that had rocked the universe. Metru Nui was in ruins, a part of the southern continent had split off and disappeared, and those were only the start of the problems. Worse, the efforts of the Brotherhood's Visorak army to conquer Metru Nui had resulted in the death of its king and the scattering of the spider creatures to points all over the map.

Nor had the Toa been sleeping through all of this. Fully aware of the depths of the Brotherhood's treachery, the Toa were striking at them at every opportunity. Brotherhood fortresses were under siege in many places. Their operations in some areas had been almost completely shut down. Granted, many Toa had been killed in the struggle – something that bothered Reidak not at all – but they had given the Brotherhood something to worry about.

Against this backdrop, the Dark Hunters'

strategy of hitting and running, sabotage, theft, and kidnapping had met with success. They had gone from annoying the Brotherhood to wounding it over the course of several hundred years. Now the Brotherhood was striking back.

Reidak peered into the darkness. Someone was moving through the woods toward the fortress. It looked to be a lone figure, too small to be an Exo-Toa, too large for a Rahkshi or a Visorak. He wondered who it might be and what kind of sound they would make when he threw them off the top of the wall.

Zaktan approached. "This one's not for you," he said. "So no mangling, shredding, or devastating."

Reidak glanced down. The figure had made it to the base of the wall impossibly fast and was already scaling the sheer stone face of it. A fleeting shaft of moonlight illuminated a sleek black form. The savage Dark Hunter grinned.

"I get it," he said. "But it would be fun to take her on someday and see which of us would end up the winner."

"You wouldn't 'end up' as anything, Reidak," a silken female voice replied. "You would just...end."

Roodaka climbed over the top of the wall. This was her third visit to this particular fortress in as many months. If the Brotherhood had known she was selling information on them to the Dark Hunters, her life would be over abruptly. Zaktan half suspected she was providing data on the Dark Hunters to the Brotherhood as well, but he couldn't prove it.

"What's the information?" he asked.

"Where's my payment?" Roodaka replied.

Zaktan handed her a tablet. Had any other Dark Hunter seen its contents, Zaktan would have been taken away immediately and imprisoned, or worse. The carving on the stone was a detailed map of the Shadowed One's fortress, complete with details on guard placement, traps, and any other security measures. With this, an enemy could sneak into the fortress and eliminate the Dark Hunter leader with ease...or so it seemed.

In fact, as Zaktan had learned the hard way, it was not so simple to overthrow the Shadowed One, even with this sort of information. If Roodaka cared to try it, she would most likely be killed, along with any other minions of the Brotherhood who went with her. If she somehow succeeded, Zaktan had no doubt he could eliminate her in turn and take power for himself.

"You need to abandon this place," Roodaka said. "It will be surrounded within the hour and overrun in two. Any Dark Hunter taken prisoner will soon wish they hadn't been."

"Why do they want this place so bad?" asked Reidak. "Besides the chance to take me out of the fight, of course."

Roodaka looked at Reidak, then turned to Zaktan. "Is he always that way?"

"Most of the time," answered Zaktan. "But he has his uses. And his question is a legitimate one – this fortress is not the most strategically located or important, so why would the Brotherhood want it so badly?"

Roodaka smiled. "Those who don't know history are doomed to repeat it, Zaktan...and sometimes, just doomed. This was a Brotherhood fortress at one time, or didn't you know?"

Zaktan cursed under his breath. No, he had not known that little piece of information, because the Shadowed One had not seen fit to tell him before sending him here.

"And I suppose you haven't explored the place, either?" Roodaka continued. "Just being good little guards, are you? Foolish, foolish pawns – what you don't know can kill you."

With a nod, she climbed back over the wall and disappeared. Zaktan stared after her, brooding. Then he said to Reidak, "Stay here. I have something to do."

"What about your part of the wall? Who's

going to watch that?"

"Isn't it obvious?" Zaktan answered. "You are. If you get overrun and killed...call me."

Before Reidak could protest any further, Zaktan headed down the stairs into the fortress. Contrary to Roodaka's belief, he had explored every inch of the place shortly after arriving. Thok had not only explored, but looted, taking anything that wasn't nailed down. But obviously they had missed something. Whatever that something was, the Brotherhood was willing to sacrifice lives to get it.

*   *   *

Thok had agreed to join Reidak on guard duty, not out of any great love of the job, but because of what Reidak had threatened to do to him if he said no. Unlike Reidak, Thok found no pleasure in fighting off the various members of the Brotherhood's army. They rarely had any treasure worth stealing or weapons worth salvaging. Besides, they took too long to die and left a mess behind.

"See anything?" asked Reidak.

"Darkness. Water. My life passing by," Thok answered.

"What's that? Out there," asked the black-armoured Piraka.

Thok sighed and took a step closer to the edge of the wall. At first, all he saw was trees and earth and ocean, here and there illuminated by a stray shaft of moonlight. Nothing out of the ordinary. A breeze was blowing through the trees, high waves were pounding the beach, and the ground was moving toward the fortress.

That last made Thok look a second time. Yes, the ground was moving...no, no, it wasn't. It was something moving along the ground — a lot of somethings. They were shrouded in mist, but their harsh chittering sounds of anticipation gave their presence away.

"Visorak!"

Dark Hunters flooded to the walls to defend the fortress, but the scene quickly devolved into chaos. Visorak Oohnorak used their power of mimicry to shout out contradictory orders in the voices of Zaktan, Ancient, and even the Shadowed One. Vohtarak made berserker charges at the base of the walls, trying to punch holes in the stone. Boggarak scaled the walls, launching their spinners and turning defenders to dust.

For their part, the Dark Hunters were mounting as strong a defense as they could. Reidak tore stones from the walls and hurled them down at the Suukorak. Thok silenced Oohnorak with his ice weapons, then tossed stones and shattered the frozen Visorak into thousands of pieces. Other Dark Hunters used spears, poles, and whatever else was handy to try and beat back the attackers.

"Much more of this and we have a problem!" Thok shouted.

"Why? Because they'll take the fortress?" said Reidak.

"No, they'll cut off our escape route," said the white-armoured Piraka. "Maybe you want to die a glorious death defending this pile of rock, but I don't. Let the rest of these losers go down as heroes in the annals of the Dark Hunters — I'll take breathing over that, any time."

"What about Zaktan?"

Thok smacked a Visorak as it edged over the wall, then grabbed the forelegs of another and hurled it into space. "What about him?" he answered.

Zaktan could hear the sounds of battle from above, but he was not about to let yet another Brotherhood attack distract him from his goal. If there was something of value to be found in this place, he would find it.

He had gone straight to the basement. It was the most likely access point for a hidden chamber, since all of the space on the upper floors was accounted for. Once down there, he performed the most thorough search possible by sending the microscopic protodites that made up his body into every crack and crevice. If they encountered a solid obstacle, he called them back. It was the ones who were able to pass through into some previously unknown room that would matter.

Zaktan could hear the shouts and screams of his Dark Hunter companions. He ignored them. His search was painstaking work and could not be rushed. It took what seemed like an eternity to find a tiny crack in the floor that led to another chamber down below. He allowed his entire body to slip through the miniscule opening and then reform in the secret sub-basement of the fortress.

At first, he was disappointed. There were no weapons or boxes of treasure anywhere about. No Kanohi masks lined the walls. He would have even settled for a second Makoki stone, but there was nothing like that, either. Just a bare room with four stone walls covered in symbols, and not even symbols that made any sense.

Still, he was in no hurry to leave. After all, going back up would just mean plunging into the middle of whatever fight was going on. So he contented himself with studying the walls and trying to get some clue to what the carvings meant.

Some of the carvings were made very forcefully, others hesitantly, and a few were violently crossed out. To Zaktan, they looked like notes of an experiment or calculations of some kind, but overall, they were gibberish. Nothing but random symbols thrown up on the wall, not forming any recognisable words or even patterns from which a code (if that was what it was) could be broken.

He took a step back and studied only the pictograms. He recognised the Great Hau mask traditionally used to symbolise the Great Spirit Mata Nui. Nearby was a carving of the Kraahkan, the mask worn by the Makuta of Metru Nui. Then there was a third symbol, one Zaktan did not recognise – it was a sharply angled crescent, the points facing upward. Intrigued, the Dark Hunter reached out and touched that symbol.

As soon as his fingers touched the crescent-shaped carving, a hum filled the room. Then to Zaktan's astonishment, the stones that made up the walls began to shift position. Slowly at first, then too rapidly for the eye to follow, they moved in and around each other, rearranging themselves to form – what?

The whole process lasted mere seconds. By the time it was done, Zaktan had retreated to the very center of the chamber for fear the walls might next attack him. In the sudden stillness that followed the remarkable display, he looked around.

It was incredible. By changing their locations on the walls, the stones had turned what was line upon line of nonsense into coherent text. Zaktan began to read, and what he read astounded him.

The chamber was a chronicle written by the Brotherhood of Makuta. It related, in detail, the events leading up to the day the Great Spirit Mata Nui fell into an eternal sleep. Zaktan had always believed that this had been a sudden event, possibly the result of some strange power of Makuta. He assumed that if the Brotherhood were to be defeated, Mata Nui would suddenly awaken.

These carvings proved him wrong. It had not been the entire Brotherhood who had done this to Mata Nui, but only one of their members — the same one who had battled the Shadowed One, and the most experienced and powerful of all the Brotherhood. And the act that resulted in Mata Nui's fall had actually taken place hundreds of years before sleep claimed him.

It was all here — the plans for Makuta's attempt to seize power in Metru Nui, prophecies about the great cataclysm, and a dire warning that the universe might end as a result of these events. There was a hastily scrawled warning about the possible coming of a Toa of Light. In one corner, there were newer carvings detailing just how long it would take for the Great Spirit to die of his injuries. At the bottom of these, a lone word was savagely inscribed in the stone: *Ignition.*

But that was far from all. No, the worst of it was staggering in its implications, blinding in its audacity...and incredible in the sheer depth of evil it revealed. The Brotherhood had predicted that, if the attempt to seize Metru Nui failed and the Matoran escaped, the villagers would eventually link up with Toa. These Toa were to be defeated if possible, but if that proved too difficult, they were to be allowed to believe they had won their ultimate battle...even if that meant the death of a Brotherhood member.

Once the Toa were sufficiently blinded by their seeming success, the true plan would unfold. When it was done, the Great Spirit would be allowed to reawaken...and a reign of darkness would begin that no Matoran ever dreamed of in his most horrifying nightmares.

Zaktan sank to the floor, stunned. What the Brotherhood was planning made the Shadowed One's schemes look like the idle fantasies of a harmless Rahi. If they were allowed to succeed, there would be no more Toa, no more Dark Hunters, just shadows and death.

His first impulse was to escape the fortress and bring all this information to someone who could act on it, even if only the Shadowed One.

That impulse lasted all of three seconds.

His second impulse made much more sense. Now that he knew all of this, somehow, someday, he would stumble on a way to be of use in this grand scheme. If he had to, he would *make* himself a part of it. And when that day came, the Brotherhood of Makuta would be in for a surprise.

They think they know evil. They think they know treachery, Zaktan thought. Then a wicked grin crawled onto his face.

Wait until they get to know me.

*   *   *

By skill and luck, the Dark Hunters managed to hold off the attack of the Visorak that night. But they all knew it would not be the last such assault. Without reinforcements, the fortress would fall.

Thok and Reidak carried through on their decision to desert. Before dawn on the morning after the battle, they slipped away, leaving the south wall unguarded. So effective was their method that none of the other Dark Hunters even knew they were gone until three dozen Rahkshi came over that wall and cut through the ranks of the defenders.

Zaktan, too, had decided it was best to be elsewhere. But before he left, he trained his impact vision on the walls of the secret chamber. Regardless of who won the battle, he wanted no one else to see this information. Let Hakann and Vezok and the rest play their little games of cross and double cross for the puniest of stakes – he would be playing for a universe.

seven

One Month Ago...

"You had better be right about this, Hakann," growled Avak, rowing through the waters of the silver sea. "Our lives depend on it."

"Then nothing of any great value is at stake," said Zaktan.

Hakann glared at the self-appointed leader of the expedition. It had been his idea to go but Zaktan who had arranged for transport and who had insisted that only the six of them – Hakann, Zaktan, Avak, Thok, Reidak, and Vezok – be informed about it. Leaving the Shadowed One's island without authorisation was punishable by death. All six had come to the conclusion that such a fate was preferable to continuing as slaves to the Dark Hunter leader.

"It's worth it," said Hakann. "Trust me."

Avak smiled. Thok chuckled. Reidak burst out laughing, followed by Vezok. "Trust you?" said Reidak, having a hard time getting the words out. "That's like a Visorak saying 'pet me.'"

"Hakann, how are we supposed to trust you?" laughed Vezok. "After all – we *know* you."

"Quiet!" snapped Zaktan. "If you cannot take this mission seriously, I will go on alone."

"No, you won't," Avak shot back. "Who would you have to order around? Yourself?" Then, noting the way the mass of protodites that made up Zaktan's body were in constant movement, he added, "Sorry. Your*selves*?"

Zaktan chose to ignore the insult. "Hakann, tell us again what you heard. Leave nothing out."

"I heard from someone who heard from someone that the Matoran are returning to Metru Nui," Hakann answered. "They are led by a group of Toa and they are planning to reclaim the city."

"Ridiculous," said Thok. "Everyone knows their Makuta drove them out of that city and won't let them return."

"I already told you," Hakann replied, smiling. "Makuta is dead and buried under a ton of rubble."

"I don't believe it," Avak said, shaking his head. "Hundreds of Dark Hunters have tried to kill him...not to mention the Toa Hagah, rebellious Visorak, and probably members of his own Brotherhood. And you're saying some handful of Toa managed to do it?"

"Well, I did leave one thing out of the story. One of the Toa was a Toa of Light."

The other Dark Hunters lapsed into shocked silence. The idea of a Toa of Light had been dismissed for centuries as just another Matoran

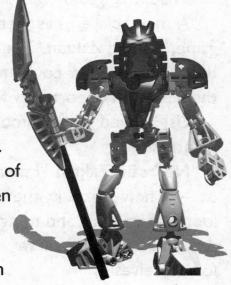

fable. The Brotherhood of Makuta had firmly stated that there was no such Toa and there never would be. These six, of course, knew differently – they had seen the Mask of Light and they knew its whereabouts had been a mystery for well over a thousand years. But the notion that it now belonged to a Toa was still an unpleasant surprise. Only Zaktan smiled inwardly, for this meant the prophecies from the fortress chamber were coming true.

"That...changes things," said Vezok.

"A new player has been added to the game," agreed Zaktan. "The Brotherhood will be panicked. This could mean the end of them...and an opportunity for us."

"Us?" asked Thok. "You mean the Dark Hunters?"

"No," said Zaktan. "I mean *us* – the six of us – a new force in the universe. We will loot Makuta's lair, and using his weapons and power, we will carve out an empire for ourselves."

"We're not Dark Hunters anymore," Vezok added. "We're what Ancient called us seven thousand years ago – we're Piraka."

"Well, whatever we are – we're here," said Avak.

The other five looked to where Avak was pointing. Just above the waterline was a stone terrace. Beyond that was an ancient gateway, now clogged with stone. If Hakann's information was correct, then past that gateway would be the remains of one of Makuta's lairs.

Avak lashed the boat to the terrace and looked around. "I don't get it. If there were Toa here, then where are they now? How did they get back out when the gate is blocked with rubble?"

"They have been on an island above," Zaktan reminded him. "There must be other ways to reach there from here. They simply used one of them."

The six Piraka climbed on to the terrace and began to clear away the rubble from the gate. It was hard work. Zaktan wanted to investigate the lair by slipping through the cracks in the rubble, but the other Piraka argued against it. Every pair of hands was needed to clear the way.

It soon became obvious that they were not just digging through random rock, but rather the shattered pieces of a huge stone door. "I don't even want to know who lifted this and then let it drop," said Avak.

"Oh, this probably wasn't that heavy," scoffed Reidak. "Wouldn't be to me, anyway."

Irritated, Thok walked over and dropped the piece of rubble he was carrying on Reidak's head. The block of stone split in two even as Reidak let out a yell of pain.

"Sorry," said Thok, smiling. "I didn't think it would be that heavy."

After a good hour of digging, Vezok said, "I found something!" The other Piraka crowded around and helped to clear away the rock. What they found stunned even such hardened, veteran Dark Hunters.

It was a black suit of armour, large and powerful-looking despite being badly damaged. The chestplate was crushed, the arm and leg armour cracked in several places, and in some places it was little more than flattened metal. The only part that seemed to have escaped damage was the Kanohi mask fitted on the headpiece. It was the Kraahkan, the legendary Mask of Shadows worn by Makuta.

"Do you think...do you think he's still alive in there?" Avak whispered.

"If he is, he soon won't be," said Zaktan. Before anyone could stop him, he reached down and pulled off the Mask of Shadows.

To his shock, there was nothing behind it but the hollow shell of the armored headpiece. He sent his protodites in through the cracks in the armour, searching for some sign of organic tissue. He found nothing. The armor was empty.

"I don't understand," said Vezok.

"Something had to make the armour move – muscle tissue – and he had to have lungs to let him breathe, and other organs. How can the armour be here, but none of that?"

The six Piraka considered the problem, each coming up with a more ghoulish theory than the last. It was Thok who finally said, "Maybe it was never there. Maybe...maybe he was just armour and energy – no organics, not anymore."

Hakann wanted to say that idea was ridiculous and impossible, but deep down, he knew it was neither. Even after a millennium of warring with them, what did any Dark Hunter really know about the members of the Brotherhood of Makuta? They were ancient, they were powerful, but beyond that, they were a mystery. Who was to say they were beings like the Piraka, the Toa, or the Matoran? Maybe they had left the need for organic tissue far behind them.

"Mask's mine," said Reidak, reaching for the Kraahkan. As soon as he touched it, the mask flared to life. A pulse of dark energy struck the Piraka, hurling him against the stone wall.

"For a mask, it has excellent taste," commented Thok.

Reidak wasn't about to give up. He grabbed the mask with both hands and held on even as it pummeled him with energy bursts. Finally, unable to withstand the pain any longer, he flung the mask off the terrace and into the sea. It disappeared beneath the waves.

"If the rest of this expedition goes that well...it will have gone really badly," said Thok. "I thought we were here to loot, not feed the fish of Metru Nui?"

Reidak cursed and the rest of the Piraka went back to work, grumbling about a potentially valuable treasure being tossed aside. None of them noticed the wisps of green vapor that hovered near the ceiling or the smoky tendrils drifting down toward them.

When the last of the rock was cleared away, they stepped into the lair itself. The place looked as if a storm had blown through it. Rahkshi cylinders were shattered and kraata were slithering all around. Chamber doors had been blasted open. Walls were scorched from both light and shadow energy bolts. Avak scouted down a corridor and reported that an entire wall at the other end had been breached, though there was no sign of what had done the job.

"Think someone got here before us?" asked Reidak.

"We will see," Zaktan replied. He pointed to the pool of energised protodermis in the center of the chamber. "Be careful not to step in that. You'll never be able to scrape it off your feet...assuming you still have feet afterward."

The initial search of the lair proved frustrating. There were notes on various Rahi experiments, half-finished pieces of equipment, and a few things that defied characterisation (worse, some of them were alive). It was Hakann who made the first potentially useful discovery in a back section of the armoury. He emerged carrying a wicked-looking spear.

"What do you think?" he asked Vezok. "The Brotherhood isn't big on close combat, so this must do something else. How do you think it works?"

"Try pointing it at someone else while you figure it out, ok?"

"What's the matter?" Hakann said, smiling. "Afraid I'll get rid of you so there's one less to share the loot with? Actually, come to think of it, that's not a bad – "

A bolt of energy shot from the point of the spear, striking Vezok. Startled, Hakann dropped the weapon. Vezok screamed. His body felt like it was being torn in two, reassembled, and then ripped apart again. He fell to the floor in agony. The other Piraka stood and watched, not sure what to do or whether they wanted to be bothered to help.

In the time it takes a heartlight to flash once, it was over. Vezok lay on the ground, groaning. And beside him, another being was rising to its feet. He had not been there a second ago, but now he stood and looked down at Vezok with contempt.

"Get up," he said. "If I can, you can — after all, I am you, and you are me, and won't that be interesting? Of course, it would be easier if there were just one of us...maybe I should die? No, no, I have that wrong — maybe you should die."

Before anyone could stop him, the newcomer snatched up the spear. He was about to use it on Vezok when he stopped. "No, no, bad idea. That will just make another of him...of me...or else something worse."

Reidak slammed into the new arrival and pinned him against the wall. "What are you? Some new trick of Makuta's? What happened to Vezok?"

"This happened," said the being calmly, hefting the spear.

Thok approached and looked at the weapon. Carved into the side of the shaft were the words *Spear of Fusion*.

"Hakann, you imbecile," he snapped. "You used it in reverse. Instead of fusing Vezok with something else, you split him into two beings! This thing is a vezon."

"A vezon?" repeated the newly created being. "Oh, yes, the Matoran word for 'double.' Yes, that does make sense. I will go by that name, then. Of course, first I will have to eliminate all of you so no one else knows I am only half a being. You don't mind, do you?"

Vezok's eyes flared to life. Thok met them and saw immediately that his fellow Piraka had changed. Gone was the cold intelligence that had kept Vezok alive all these years, replaced by white-hot anger. Vezok roared and threw himself at Vezon, wrestling with him for the spear. When Reidak tried to intervene, Vezok lashed out and knocked the Piraka to the ground.

Zaktan dissolved his body into a flying swarm of protodites. He flew in between the two combatants, blinding them and cutting off their air. Both backed off, choking, but Vezon still held on to the spear.

Zaktan would later recall that this was the

moment all had become clear to him. He didn't know how or why, but suddenly he realised that they had come to this place for a reason. There was something they had to find, but it wasn't here. It was elsewhere, on an island far to the south, and hidden in a place of fire. It was powerful, old beyond even the universe itself, and it was waiting for them.

"The Mask of Life," he said softly. A thrill went through him, for he knew this was the moment he had been waiting for. A doorway into the Brotherhood's plan had suddenly opened and he was going to step inside.

"The Mask of – " Thok began. Then he stopped, startled that Zaktan had evidently read his thoughts.

"Think what we could do with that," said Avak. "Think what it must be worth!"

Hakann said nothing. He was calculating how many Piraka would be needed to retrieve such a mask, and how quickly he could eliminate them once it was in their possession.

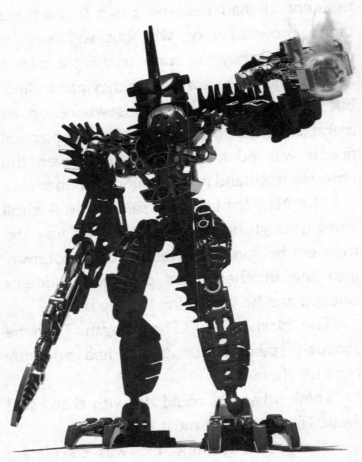

Even Vezok forgot his rage for a moment. The image of the mask filled his mind. It was no mere Kanohi. It was a key in the same way that the Makoki stone had been a key — but a key to all of existence.

"Find it. We have to find it," he muttered.

"I agree," said Vezon.

All six turned to look at him. The fury was already returning to Vezok's eyes. This time, Reidak succeeded in getting between them. "Let him help," he said to Vezok in a harsh whisper. "And if he dies in the process...so what? No big loss. He shouldn't be alive in the first place."

"No," said Zaktan. "We have no room for a seventh, especially one with such a strange origin."

"You should talk," said Reidak. "Vezok knows better than to betray his partners. I'm betting Vezon does, too. Now, do you want to spend who knows how long trying to get that spear away from him, or do you want to invite him along?"

"He's right, for once," said Thok. "A battle might leave none of us in any shape to hunt for the mask."

Reluctantly, Zaktan agreed. It was urgent

they find the Mask of Life. He knew that as surely as he knew his own name. There was no time for arguments.

"We are done here," he said. "We must head to the island home of the mask immediately."

"I know you're right," said Avak. "But... isn't there more we should take from here? The mask has been hidden for thousands of years... why do we have to rush?"

No one had an answer for him. They just knew they had to make best speed to the island of Voya Nui. If any thought it strange that they now knew the name of an island none had ever heard of before, no one chose to say so aloud.

"You know, there's only one thing bothering me," said Reidak, looking around. "All this stuff – a Makuta lair, of all places – and there's no one and nothing here on guard. Doesn't that seem kind of weird?"

Reidak's answer was an explosion that threw all seven Piraka against the far wall.

When the smoke cleared, they could see that an entire section of the lair was gone, disintegrated with one blast. Something moved in the shadows...something huge.

"Makuta?" said Hakann, already planning his escape route.

"Don't be stupid," hissed Avak. "Makuta's dead. At worst, it's some Toa with more power than sense, and — "

The shape emerged from the shadows. It was massive. Eyes perched high in a red and yellow head regarded the Piraka with total disdain, as if they were insects infesting this being's home. Its body was rectangular and blocky in shape, with two powerful arms and thick legs that ended in a solid band of armour. At both ends of the band were treads that rolled over the rubble with ease.

"Mana Ko," whispered Zaktan, stunned.

"Huh?" said Reidak.

"The Brotherhood uses crablike creatures called Manas as guardians," Zaktan explained hurriedly. "I once saw them wipe out a dozen

Dark Hunters in a matter of minutes. The Brotherhood always said they were just a sample — that the real power was the Mana Ko. This matches the description."

"Ok, so it's a Rahi," Reidak shrugged. "A really big Rahi...ok, a gigantic Rahi...that can blow away walls. Let's just get in our boat and leave."

As if it understood what the Piraka was saying, the Mana Ko aimed a second blast at the stone terrace. It crumbled and fell into the sea, right on top of where the Piraka's boat had been moored.

"Then again, why leave when it's just getting exciting?" said Reidak.

"We will have to fight," said Zaktan. "Vezon, you distract the monster, and we will — where's Vezon?"

The other Piraka looked around. Their newest "ally" had disappeared, taking the spear with him.

"He got Vezok's brains all right," Avak muttered. "And Hakann's courage, from the look of it."

"Split up," Zaktan ordered. "Otherwise, one blast kills us all."

"Yes," said Thok, already on the move. "By all means, let's make it fire at least six times."

"Imprison that thing, Avak," Zaktan ordered.

Avak concentrated. A prison that appeared to be made of clear glass materialised around the Mana Ko. When the beast unleashed another blast, it reflected off the walls and ricocheted all over the inside of the cage. One such experience was enough for the monstrous Rahi, which responded with a keening wail.

"Keep it caged until we are on our way out of here," said Zaktan. "The rest of you, find us a way out of here – and find Vezon!"

The Piraka had barely begun to grumble about who should be giving orders and who should be taking them when the wall behind them exploded inward. A flying piece of masonry slammed into Avak, knocking him flat. In an instant, the prison around the Mana Ko dissolved.

Thok didn't want to look and see the source of the second explosion. He really didn't. He knew that, whatever it was, he wasn't going to want to see it. In fact, it might well ruin what was turning out to be possibly the last day of his life.

He looked anyway. A second Mana Ko was coming from behind them. The Piraka were trapped between the two Rahi.

I cannot believe this, thought Thok. *Yesterday, I was a Dark Hunter — respected, hated, and feared. Today I am about to be destroyed by angry seafood.*

"How come there's never a Toa around when you need one?" asked Reidak.

"What, to save us?" asked Thok.

"No, to die first," Reidak replied. "We might as well get some fun out of this trip."

Both Mana Ko had stopped dead, as if waiting to see what the Piraka would do. Hakann stuck his head up over the rubble and waved his arm. One of the Mana Ko responded with a blast that blew a large hole in a side wall.

"They react to movement," he reported.

"So all we have to do is stay still and do absolutely nothing. In other words, have a normal day for Thok."

"We have two choices — fight or run," said Zaktan.

"You forgot the third option — die horribly," said Thok.

"Movement, huh?" said Vezok. "Okay, on the count of three, we make for that hole they just blew in the wall. One...two..."

The blue-armoured Piraka suddenly grabbed Hakann and threw him out into the open. Both Mana Ko turned in Hakann's direction.

"Three!" shouted Vezok, leading the dash for the gap, followed closely by all of the others except Hakann.

Both Mana Ko blasted at the crimson-armoured Piraka at the same time. He ducked, dove, and rolled, trying to avoid being shattered into more pieces than Zaktan. Between explosions, he looked up to see the receding backs of his partners. He made a vow to get even with Vezok. He wasn't so much angry at what Vezok had done as he was at himself for not thinking of it first.

Something was sticking out of the rubble just ahead. He grabbed it and pulled it free, finding it was a broken piece of Makuta's armour. Giving a yell, he hurled it behind him. When the two Mana Ko reacted by attacking the moving object, Hakann scrambled for the hole his partners had gone through.

They hadn't made it very far. The chamber the Piraka had found themselves in was a dead end.

"Now what?" growled Reidak. "Can't go forward, can't go back."

Thok frowned. "Well, I think we should – "

"Watch out!"

All five turned to see Hakann running toward them, the Mana Ko right behind.

"Idiot!" snapped Zaktan. "You were supposed to stay in there and keep them occupied."

"I did," yelled Hakann. "And it was so much

fun, I want you all to have a turn!"

"This could be a good thing," said Thok. "Everybody hit the ground! Now!"

All six Piraka dove to the stone floor. The Mana Ko hurled lethal blasts of energy, blowing apart the back wall.

"Now run!" shouted Thok.

The pursuit that followed was a bizarre one, even for ex-Dark Hunters. As each corridor ended in a blank wall, the two Mana Ko would obligingly blast a new exit in their effort to destroy the Piraka. The path turned into a steep and narrow incline, forcing the Piraka to move faster. Bunched up as they were, one good blast would down them all. Then Zaktan noticed something extremely odd. The Mana Ko had stopped advancing. They were standing at the bottom of the incline, just watching. Victory was in their grasp, but it seemed like there was now some invisible barrier between them and the Piraka.

"Why aren't they attacking?" asked Hakann. "We're sitting Gukko here."

"I don't know. I don't care," answered Zaktan. "That wall up ahead — we'll bring it down."

The two Piraka joined with Vezok to strike at the wall with their vision powers. It took far longer than they expected to cut a hole through it, but when they did, they found themselves in another world.

Incredibly bright and hot sunlight poured down on them from an impossibly blue sky. A salty sea breeze set tropical trees to swaying, while brakas monkeys chased sea birds that flew too close to the branches. The air was alive with the sounds of Rahi and the crash of the distant surf against the rocks.

It was truly disgusting.

"Too bright!" griped Reidak, shading his eyes. "Who could live like this?"

"Smell the air," Thok said, his face clenching like a fist. "It's...vile."

"I'd rather be back with the Mana Ko," Avak muttered. "What kind of pesthole is this?"

Zaktan wasn't listening. He was looking around, noting that the six Piraka were standing in what appeared to be a natural temple. A huge mountain towered over them. Carved into it was an image Zaktan recognised as being that of the legendary Mask of Light.

He dissolved into a swarm of protodites and drifted up into the sky. From that vantage point, he could see distant villages, all of them empty. The beach was littered with pieces of wood and a few half-finished boats. There was not a Matoran or a Toa to be seen anywhere.

Then the rumours were true, Zaktan said to himself. *After the cataclysm, the Matoran of Metru Nui fled beyond the sky...and now they are returning to their home.*

He remembered the sudden reluctance of the Mana Ko to pursue. They must have had orders from Makuta, he reasoned. If they had come to this island, not a Matoran would have been left alive. Makuta wanted to rule them, not kill them, so he kept his monsters on a leash.

As he descended to bring this news to his partners, Zaktan's eyes spotted something else. Six large canisters rested on their ends in a row near the base of the mountain. They had obviously been placed there for a reason. Their condition showed that someone had been tasked with taking care of them.

It took only a short examination for him to determine that these were Toa transport canisters. He had no idea to whom they belonged, nor did it matter, as long as those Toa were nowhere around. With their boat destroyed by the Mana Ko, these would be a perfect solution to the problem of getting to Voya Nui.

Then an idea struck Zaktan. There would almost certainly be Matoran where the Piraka were going. And what Matoran would not hail the arrival of Toa canisters, and the Toa they inevitably brought? Traveling in these would give an invader a free pass to almost any island.

He smiled. Even if the Piraka could only fool the Matoran into thinking they were Toa for a brief time, those few hours or days might be all they would need to find the Mask of Life.

Within the hour, the Piraka had succeeded in hauling the canisters down to the beach. Avak had managed to figure out how they worked and chart a rough course to Voya Nui, with Zaktan's help. Neither wasted time wondering how they knew just where the island was located. There was, after all, a mask to find.

"When we get there, remember – you are Toa," Zaktan said. "Try to act like them...or at least not like your usual selves. The Matoran will welcome us as heroes, little suspecting our true natures."

"That's right," laughed Reidak. "Hey, look at me! I'm Toa Reidak! Where's my mask? Where's my tool? Where's my swelled head and stuck-up attitude?"

Zaktan frowned. "Perhaps, Reidak, it would be better if you stay in your canister and let the Matoran come to you. It might be more convincing."

One by one, the Piraka climbed into their canisters. Hakann helped Vezok into his and watched as the hatch was sealed. When he was sure no one was looking, he used two quick bursts of his heat vision to puncture a tiny hole in the canister and weld the hatch shut.

I'm not sure if you can swim, Vezok, old friend, Hakann thought. *But I'll bet you can drown.*

The six canisters moved away from the beach. Each Piraka knew now that there was no turning back. They had abandoned their lives as Dark Hunters and would, now, be actively hunted down as traitors by their former comrades. They were embarking on a new adventure – a chance to steal a mask coveted for ages by powerful factions throughout the universe. If they succeeded in their mission, they would be at war with the world. If they failed, they would be dead.

As their canisters rode the waves southward, none of the Piraka could picture a life better than this.

epilogue

Today...

Zaktan's reminiscences ceased. Amazingly, he had sifted through all these tales and memories in a matter of a few seconds. The staircase awaited, and at its end, everything he had ever wanted: ultimate power and the chance for revenge.

He had no doubt Vezon had already passed this way. Thok and Reidak had discovered a canister on another part of the Voya Nui beach, one that had not belonged to the Piraka or the Toa Inika. Where Vezon got it, he had no idea, but the tracks leading away from it definitely belonged to their short-lived ally.

Vezon found his way here — I am not sure how I know, but I know, Zaktan thought. *But he did not get away with the Mask of Life. If he had... somehow I would know that, too. He is still down there...waiting for us.*

Zaktan slowed his pace, allowing Hakann to pass him. He would grant the crimson-armoured Piraka the privilege of leading the way – and the privilege of being the first to encounter whatever lethal guardians might block their passage. With any luck, Hakann would be ashes long before they ever reached the mask chamber.

Seven thousand years, he said to himself. *I have known these five, fought with and beside them, and faced horrors in their company for all that time. It has all led up to this one day and this final crime.*

Six Piraka descend the stairs...but only one will return. And that one will be me.

Zaktan suddenly paused. For a moment... only a moment...he thought he heard laughter. It wasn't coming from behind them or before them, but rather it was in his own mind. He heard it as clearly as he heard his own thoughts, which just made the experience that much more disturbing.

For the laughter was not his own....

Thok watched Hakann disappear into the darkness. He could guess why Zaktan had allowed him to go on ahead. It was the same reason Thok was purposely walking slowly and lagging behind. He had no intention of turning his back on any of the other Piraka, let alone being first in line to get devoured by whatever lurked here.

He could hear Hakann's steady footsteps up ahead as he went down the stone stairs. There was something comforting in the noise. After all, if he was proceeding at a normal pace, he must not have encountered any obstacles or foes.

Maybe Vezon took care of all of them for us, he thought, smiling.

Such happy thoughts were driven out of his mind by a yell from Avak. He had almost tripped over the battered body of Hakann.

The crimson-armoured Piraka was huddled in a corner, trembling with fear. His armour was glowing with such intense heat that no one could even come near him, let alone touch him. The metal was literally melting before their eyes, but there was nothing to suggest a reason for it.

Then Thok realised that he could still hear the measured footsteps up ahead, the ones he had originally thought were Hakann's. They were moving at the same unhurried pace as before, one after the other in an unceasing pattern. The only problem was, they weren't going down the stairs.

They were coming up.

BIONICLE®

Bring the legends to life - don't miss the other great BIONICLE® books.

BIONICLE® CHRONICLES

Tale of the Toa (978-0-00-723188-1)
Beware the Bohrok (978-0-00-723189-8)
Makuta's Revenge (978-0-00-723190-4)
Tales of the Masks (978-0-00-723191-1)

BIONICLE® Legends

Island of Doom (978-0-00-724626-7)
Dark Destiny (978-0-00-724627-4)
Power Play (978-0-00-724628-1)
Legacy of Evil (978-0-00-724631-1)